Cardinal and Sunflower

BY JAMES PRELLER

PICTURES BY HUY VOUN LEE

HARPERCOLLINS*PUBLISHERS*

Special thanks to Charles Walcott, the Louis Agassiz Fuertes Director
of the Cornell Laboratory of Ornithology, for kindly reading an early draft of the
manuscript, providing both insight and encouragement. Special notice must
also go out to a useful little book called AMERICA'S FAVORITE BACKYARD BIRDS by Kit
and George Harrison. In it I discovered their transcription of the cardinal
song—"What cheer! What cheer! Birdie, birdie, birdie. Cue, cue, cue, cue!"—
and I was on my way. And lastly, thanks to Dad, who always had bird
feeders in the backyard, and a handy bird book nearby.
—J.P.

Cardinal and Sunflower
Text copyright © 1998 by James Preller
Illustrations copyright © 1998 by Huy Voun Lee
Printed in the U.S.A. All rights reserved.

Library of Congress Cataloging-in-Publication Data
Preller, James.
    Cardinal and sunflower / by James Preller ; pictures by Huy Voun Lee.
        p.   cm.
    Summary: The seeds scattered by a mother and her child as they walk through the park on
a cold winter day feed a pair of cardinals and grow into a plant that feeds their babies the
next summer.
    ISBN 0-06-026222-2.
    [1. Cardinals (Birds)—Fiction.   2. Sunflowers—Fiction.]   I. Lee, Huy Voun, ill.   II. Title.
PZ7.P915Car 1998   97-11646
[E]—dc21   CIP
                                                                                                                    AC

Typography by Alicia Mikles
1 2 3 4 5 6 7 8 9 10
❖
First Edition
Visit us on the World Wide Web!
http://www.harperchildrens.com

To Drs. Andre Lascari, Jennifer Pearce, and
Joanne Porter—and to RNs Judith Doell, Cathy Ives,
Janis Koshgarian, and Kari VanDenburgh—
for your unfailing compassion, care, and skill.
—J.P.

For my brother, Chin, who gave the
sunflower, and for my sister, Mong,
who invested in me.
—H.V.L.

Come see a mother and child,
bundled up against the cold,
take a winter stroll through the park,
tossing sunflower seeds as they go.

Now watch as a gathering of birds,
spied by two gray squirrels,
squabble over the last handful of seeds.

In courtship, a gallant cardinal
cracks open a seed with his hard beak.
He tenderly places the sweet nut
into his mate's red-brown bill.

He spies an old tomcat
and cries a sharp "*chip, chip.*"
As one, the birds take wing across the sky.
Only a few scattered seeds remain.

The cold of winter gives way
to the warmth of spring.
Small buds appear on the trees.
The grass returns, pale green and tender to eat.
People begin to fill the park,
dressed in bright colors.

And in one secret place,
a fragile shoot reaches for the sky.

The female cardinal senses the change in season.
She selects a thicket and weaves bark strips,
rootlets, and twigs into a bowl-shaped nest.
Finally she lines the inside of the nest
with soft, fine grasses.
It is ready.
Upon a branch, the male sings out,
"*What cheer! What cheer!*
Birdie, birdie, birdie.
Cue, cue, cue, cue!"

One, two, three, four speckled eggs
fill the nest.

The father brings seeds, cracked corn,
grasshoppers, and grubs to the mother.
Steady and fierce, she protects the nest
from preying blue jays and black crows.

Now come days of rain, nights of rain.

Squirrels sit in trees,

tails curled over their backs like umbrellas.

People hurry past, jumping over puddles.

Roots drink deep.

A stem grows thick and tall.

On the thirteenth day of waiting,
the mother hears low, rhythmic tapping.
She cocks her head and listens
for small cheeps from inside the eggs.
She answers with a soft call of her own.
"*What cheer. What cheer,*" she whispers.
"*Birdie, birdie, birdie.*
Love, love, love, love."

Now the days come clear and easy.

Ripe strawberries crowd the bushes.

Striped chipmunks scamper beneath the willows.

A black dog leaps high

and snatches a Frisbee from the air.

And in one secret place,
where birds once plucked seeds from the ground,
a solitary sunflower lifts its golden head
to greet the wind and clouds and trees and sun.
It says, *I am.*

Four new chicks,
born blind and helpless,
instinctively open their orange-pink gullets
to the sky.

Father and mother work feverishly
to feed their young, who cry in hunger,
"*Feed us, feed us, feed us, feed us.*"

Soon comes the first day of flight.
With food dangling from their beaks,
both parents perch a few feet away
and call to their hungry chicks.
"*Fly here! Fly Here!*
Birdie, birdie, birdie.
Come, come, come, come."

In little leaps and bounds
the chicks chase after fat worms. . . .
And learn to fly.

Satisfied that her chicks are healthy and strong,
the mother cardinal grows restless once more.
She knows there is yet
a second clutch of eggs to lay,
a second brood to care for and feed.
She leaves to build a new nest.

The red-crested father remains
for a few days with the chicks,
now nearly full grown.
They follow their father
to learn how to find food and shelter.

Together they discover the miracle—
a yellow sun that has risen from the ground.
"*What cheer! What cheer!*" they sing.
The birds feast until their bird-bellies are full.

And a mother and child,
now warmed by the sun,
take a summer stroll through the park,
tossing sunflower seeds as they go.